RHONDA
GOWLER
GREENE

illustrated by
HENRY
COLE

SANTA'S
STUCK

DUTTON CHILDREN'S BOOKS
NEW YORK

Text copyright © 2004 by Rhonda Gowler Greene
Illustrations copyright © 2004 by Henry Cole

LIBRARY OF CONGRESS CATALOGING-IN-PUBLICATION DATA
Greene, Rhonda Gowler.
Santa's stuck / by Rhonda Gowler Greene;
illustrated by Henry Cole.—1st ed.
p. cm.
Summary: When Santa becomes stuck in the
chimney of a house on Christmas Eve, the dog,
the cat, the reindeer, and a mouse try to free him.
ISBN 0-525-47292-4
1. Santa Claus—Juvenile fiction. [1. Santa Claus—
Fiction. 2. Christmas—Fiction. 3. Animals—Fiction.
4. Stories in rhyme.] I. Title: Santa is stuck.
II. Cole, Henry, ill. III. Title.
PZ8.3.G824San 2004   [E]—dc22   2003062613

Published in the United States
by Dutton Children's Books,
a division of Penguin Young Readers Group
345 Hudson Street, New York, New York 10014
www.penguin.com/youngreaders

Designed by Heather Wood
Manufactured in China
3 5 7 9 10 8 6 4

For Matt, Aaron,
Lianna, and Brad . . .
Merry Christmas!
Love, Mom

—R.G.G.

For W.J.A.

—H.C.

Toys are nestled, tree lights glow.
Stockings, stuffed, march in a row.
Santa sighs. It's time to go . . .

Dear Santa,
We have been
very good

Gathers up his giant sack,
spies a note and Christmas snack!

Boys and girls have been so kind.
They left sweets for him to find.
Hmm . . . his suit feels rather snug.
Santa shrugs a jolly shrug.
One more cookie? Couldn't hurt.
This last snack will be—dessert!

Santa rests his weary feet,
munches on a scrumptious treat.
Nibble, nibble. Tasty crumbs!
Licks the frosting from his thumbs.
Smacks his lips on fruitcake, too.
Wolfs the whole thing!
Chomp chomp chew.

Chocolate fudge!
He sneaks a piece.
Can't resist . . .
He has a feast!

Belly bulges. Santa stops.
Uh-oh! Look! A button *pops!*

Restless reindeer. Cold wind blows . . .
Up the chimney, Santa goes . . .

Suddenly, a sound is heard—
rap-tap-tap—and one wee word:
"Help!"

Little ones tucked in their beds,
candy-cane dreams in their heads,
slumber on, don't hear a peep . . .
but dog bolts upright from his sleep.

Bravely *pit-pats* down the stair,
sees boots kicking in the air!

Santa whispers, "I'm stuck tight."
Dog helps—*push!*—with all his might.
No-o-o-o-o luck—
Santa's stuck!

Meanwhile, reindeer heed the plea,
form a chain, then pull on three.

One . . . two . . . three!
Dasher, Dancer, Prancer, Vixen,
Comet, Cupid, Donder, Blitzen—
Rudolph, too. They all heave-ho
as one dog pushes down below.

No-o-o-o-o luck—
Santa's stuck!

Help!

Mama cat wakes from her nap,
hears that "Help!" and *rap-tap-tap*.
Sees that Santa's in a fix,
calls her kittens, one through six:
One . . . two . . . three . . .
Four . . . five . . . six . . . Meow!

Reindeer, dog, kittens, cat . . .
pull like this . . . push like that . . .
No-o-o-o-o luck—
Santa's stuck!

Ho-ho-ho! A tiny mouse
stirs inside his tiny house.

Go!

Scampers out to lend a hand . . .
Santa gives the "GO!" command.

Pu-u-u-ush . . .
pu-u-u-ull . . .
Pu-u-u-ush . . .
pu-u-u-ull . . .

POP!

Santa's out! A silent cheer!

Reindeer harness up their gear.

Back inside his Christmas sleigh,
Santa shouts, "Now dash away!"

Then he waves and soars from sight—
"Merry Christmas and good night!"